ERICA'S ELEPHANT

TRONK

Scholastic Children's Books
An imprint of Scholastic Ltd
Euston House, 24 Eversholt Street,
London, NW1 1DB, UK
Registered office: Westfield Road, Southam, Warwickshire, CV47 0RA
SCHOLASTIC and associated logos are trademarks and/or
registered trademarks of Scholastic Inc.

First published in the UK by Scholastic Ltd, 2016

Text copyright © Sylvia Bishop, 2016
Illustrations © Ashley King, 2016

The rights of Sylvia Bishop and Ashley King to be identified
as the author and illustrator of this work respectively have
been asserted by them.

ISBN 978 1407 16829 6

Printed by CPI Group (UK) Ltd, Croydon, CR0 4YY
Papers used by Scholastic Children's Books are made from wood
grown in sustainable forests.

1 3 5 7 9 10 8 6 4 2

This is a work of fiction. Names, characters, places, incidents
and dialogues are products of the author's imagination or are used
fictitiously. Any resemblance to actual people, living or dead,
events or locales is entirely coincidental.

www.scholastic.co.uk

SCHOLASTIC

ERICA'S ELEPHANT

▶▶▶◀◀▶▶▶◀◀◀▶▶◀◀◀▶▶▶◀◀◀

SYLVIA BISHOP

Illustrated by Ashley King

For my parents, with all my love,
and a heartfelt **TRONK**

Jasmine ♡

The First Chapter:
In which the Elephant arrives

The Elephant was on Erica's doorstep on the morning of her tenth birthday. There was also a piece of paper stating that she, Erica Perkins, had a Legal Right to the Elephant. "But it's all very well," said Erica, "fussing about whether I have a Right to the Elephant. The Elephant has been Left to me, and that seems to be the bigger problem." She looked the

Elephant in the eye. "Who left you?" she demanded. "And why?"

TRONK, said the Elephant. It seemed to Erica to be the sort of **TRONK** which said, *I am the wrong elephant to ask. I am*

confused by life in general and your doorstep in particular.

She felt a little sorry for the Elephant, **TRONK**ing on the step with no idea why he was there or who had sent him, so she patted him on the trunk and led him inside. He broke the door frame, but **TRONK**ed so sadly about it that Erica wasn't even cross. Besides, it wasn't really his fault. The house was certainly not built for a fine, big elephant like him. It was a two-up, two-down terraced house by the coast, with nice views of the sea but very little space.

Erica had lived in that house for as long as she could remember. At first she had shared it with Uncle Jeff, who was the only family she had. He meant well, but he was very distracted, and he usually forgot that she was there. He was an ornithologist, which means he studied birds, and he was forever thinking about birds and where he could go to see them and what sort of binoculars he ought to take. Erica had to do all the practical things like cooking and cleaning the house. When she was eight he left to hunt for a bird called the Lesser Pip-footed Woob. He had left some money in an envelope to last until his return, but here she was two years later, with only £30.42 left and no word from Uncle Jeff.

And now there was an elephant in her house.

"Well," she said, "I suppose you can have Uncle Jeff's room."

TRONK, said the Elephant. This time the meaning was a bit unclear, but Erica thought he sounded confused about what an unclejeffsroom was, and unsure about whether it was a good thing to have. She sighed. He was not going to be an easy house guest to look after.

For a start, she didn't know what elephants like to eat. While the Elephant explored the unclejeffsroom, discovering which bits were strong and which made satisfying CRACK noises when stamped on, she looked it up online. Any plants would do, she learned – cabbage was a good bet – but he would need 150 kilograms of it a day. You or I might eat, say, two kilograms of food a day. 150 kilograms is rather a lot of cabbage. Erica was a very practical girl, and she thought about the

Lorenzo

£30.42 that she had left, and the cost of cabbage, and did a quick sum.

Upstairs, the Elephant discovered a mirror and started **TRONK**ing in terror. Erica had already sighed, and as she was a very practical girl she knew there

was no point sighing again, so she went out to the garden to see what greenery she could collect as a snack.

By the time she came back in with the final bag full of grass, leaving the garden lawn bare, the Elephant had tired himself out and was taking a nap. She left the food in his doorway and went back to bed with a book. Sometimes that is the best response to life.

Rain was battering the roof. The sound was comfortingly normal, and seemed to say that there was nothing she could do about the Elephant Question while the weather was so bad, and she might as well stay warm in her duvet. Suddenly, mixed in with the rain, she heard the THUMP of shy Elephant steps. They came closer, then went away again. She got up and opened the door.

There was a stuffed puffin in the doorway. It was one of the horrible stuffed birds that Uncle Jeff kept in his bedroom. It lay on its back with its feet in the air, one glass eye fixed on Erica, the other on the Elephant – as if by watching both of them at once, it could work out what was going on. The Elephant looked down at his trunk and flicked his tail around nervously. **TRONK**?

"I don't understand," said Erica.

The Elephant thought about this. He

went into his room, used his trunk to hook up one of the bags she had used for grass, and set it down next to the bird. He carefully placed the bird in the bag, and the bag at Erica's feet. **TRONK**?

"Oh!" she said. "You're bringing me dinner?"

He nodded, ears flapping.

"Ah." There was nothing she could say to that which didn't seem rude or ungrateful, so she settled for a noise: a sort of "Mmmmharrrhm". And then, when this didn't seem to reassure him, she said, "Well. Thank you... That's very... Thank you."

Now, the Elephant was not stupid. There was a lot he didn't know, but that is not the same thing at all. He knew perfectly well that "Mmmmharrrhm" and "That's very…" did not mean that Erica liked the bird. A little sheepishly, he hooked up the bag and took it back to the unclejeffsroom with a sorry **Tronk**.

"No, really, thank you!" Erica called after him. "I mean, I can't eat it. But it really was very nice of you." She thought she heard him sigh, but she had never heard an elephant sigh before, so it was difficult to tell. He didn't come out again that evening.

The next day a postcard was lying on the mat, showing a building topped with what looked like ice-cream dollops made of white stone. It read:

Dear ~~Erika~~ Erica,

I am sending you an elephant! It was giving rides to tourists but had hurt its knee so they were getting rid of it cheap. Hope you like it!

All well here. No sign of the Woob yet but I did see an Emerald Sprik. In these winter months they shed all their feathers and hibernate in the mountains to think about maths problems – so I was very lucky to spot one.

Yours fondly,

Uncle Jeff

TAJ MAHAL, AGRA, UTTAR PRADESH, INDIA

She turned the postcard over a few times, as if hoping to find the part she had missed, where Jeff said when he was coming home or what to do about money or how to look after an elephant. The postcard stubbornly continued not to say any of these things. **TAJ MAHAL, AGRA,**

UTTAR PRADESH, INDIA, said the small type at the bottom. Which was not, as such, helpful.

Whenever Erica felt a bit lost – which wasn't often – she went for a walk to the end of the pier to clear her head. She went there now, first tip-tapping down the pavements and then crunching along the stony beach, while the wind did its best to tug her sideways, like an annoying younger brother that you are quite fond of really.

On the pier she leant against the railings and watched the back-and-forward of the sea. For a while she didn't think anything at all, and then eventually she thought these three things:

1. I am so glad that whenever I am in
   a Tricky Situation, everything here is
   Familiar and Soothing.
2. It must be horribly hard to be
   in a Tricky Situation when you
   are somewhere Strange and Unknown.
3. Oh. It is probably quite hard to find
   yourself on an Unknown Doorstep
   with a bad knee, in a world where
   things are so Strange that you can't
   even get someone dinner without
   making a fool of yourself.

After she had thought these three
things, she crunched to the tourist office,
filled her rucksack with free leaflets, and
tip-tapped back home to the Elephant.

When she went upstairs, he was sitting looking out of Uncle Jeff's window, trunk scrunched up against the glass. Erica coughed. The Elephant, puzzled by the greeting, coughed back to be on the safe side.

"Do you like the view?" she asked.

He **TRONK**ed politely.

"You're in England," she said.

The Elephant blinked.

"That's the sea you were looking at just now." She started pulling the leaflets out of her bag and spreading them out on the carpet, lining them up like a game of solitaire. "We're very close to it. And we're right by the Pavilion, where the Prince used to live. We could visit that ... although I'm not sure they'd let you inside... Anyway. I just thought I'd talk you through it all. Look, here's a map: this is us." She pointed to the squiggle that stood for her road. Then she traced her finger around the curves of her town, stopping at every major landmark to open a leaflet and show him the pictures. He ran his trunk in wonder over the fish at the aquarium, the bright white of the pier, the impossible soaring carts of the Ferris wheel.

When they had looked at all the leaflets, she pulled an atlas from the bookcase and showed him where they were in England, and where England was in the world. The scale of the world seemed to puzzle him.

Erica watched him flip from the map of Britain to the map of the world and back again with his trunk, as if he was trying to understand how something which took up a whole page could possibly be so small.

"Shall we go for a walk?" said Erica, when he had tired of the maps. "What would you like to see?"

The Elephant looked from leaflet to leaflet in great uncertainty. He looked out of the window at the glinting sea, and back at the leaflets, and at Erica, and for a while at the ceiling. At last, he jerked his head towards the window with a hopeful **TRONK**.

"The sea? Of course."

And so Erica and the Elephant pattered

and crashed down the stairs, and tip-tapped and thumped along the pavements, and crunched along the beach. The Elephant's steps were a little uneven. It seemed his knee had not quite recovered.

The beach was made of pebbles, not sand, and the wintry sea air was biting at their skin. The Elephant didn't seem to mind. It was obvious that he adored the sea. Erica showed him her favourite game: wading out a little, waiting for a wave to roll in, then trying to jump high enough to clear it. He was very, very bad at the game – elephants cannot jump – but he would earnestly watch each wave with a worried squint, and then stagger about with a loud **TRONK** of victory, believing

he had done very well. She began to feel rather fond of him.

To get to the main road from the beach, they had to climb up using one of the sets of metal steps that were set into the wall, spaced out along the shore. Erica tripped over the final step, turning her ankle to one side as she fell. She was a very practical girl, so she got up and dusted herself off, but a nasty twinge in her ankle turned her tip-tapping into more of a *ti*-TUM, *ti*-TUM.

The Elephant watched her in alarm, and after she had limped on for a few steps, he blocked her path and knelt down in front of her. **TRONK**, he said: *Get on.*

"No," she said, "you have a bad knee."

He flapped his ears and **TRONK**ed angrily. For the first time, Erica realized how powerful he was, and for a moment she was almost afraid of him. But he wasn't really angry with *her*, just very unhappy about something else. **TRONK**, he repeated, firmly but more kindly. *I'm fine.*

So Erica got on the Elephant's back, and hung on for dear life as he tottered to his feet again (elephants are not well designed for standing up, and they are very clumsy about it). They swayed back home, the Elephant finding the way with a proud THUMP and a very slight limp, pausing to take bites out of people's hedges here and there. Erica decided to explain "front garden" and "private" some other time; it had already been a big day. Besides, she had something much more important to explain, which she had been putting off ever since the postcard had arrived that morning.

She put it off all through the Elephant's

first viewing of The News on the TV (which he didn't like at all), and then put it off some more while showing him how to make tea (which he liked once he had got used to the way the kettle jigged around towards the end). But when he started yawning the most enormous YAWNs, she knew she couldn't put it off any longer. She fetched one last leaflet from her bag. It read:

THE SEABREEZE ZOO
A great day out for everyone!

This was stamped over a picture of a roaring lion, who was presumably having a Great Day Out. Erica put the leaflet on the table. "We need to talk," she said.

Now, humans know that "We need to talk" means "I am about to say something difficult", but elephants don't. The Elephant's **TRONK** was curious, but not worried.

She took a deep breath. "I can't afford to feed you."

The Elephant looked politely interested.

"Do you understand? Your food costs money. I don't have any. I'm really sorry."

The Elephant tried and failed to hide a yawn. Erica, being a very practical girl, saw that they would be there all night if she didn't say it very plainly. "You can't stay here."

The Elephant reeled in his trunk in shock, and blinked. He looked at Erica. She looked at him. A fly crawling down the window stopped in its tracks and looked at both of them.

"I'm so sorry," she said. "Really I am. But you'd starve here. Look" – she held up the leaflet – "I found somewhere you could stay, where they could feed you. There's a whole enclosure full of elephants!" The Elephant looked puzzled. "Enclosure? Er..." said Erica, "well, it means... It's a place you can stay! But you can't – well..." She was a very honest girl, but this was a difficult sort of thing to tell him. "The thing with an enclosure is, you can't leave it. But it's *nice* there."

At this, the Elephant draped an ear over his eyes and refused to look at her. She read the leaflet out loud to him, but he stayed firmly behind his ear, not showing any interest in the Wild Child Play Area or the One-stop Tiptop Treetop

Gift Shop. When she had finished reading there was a long silence.

She put her palm on his trunk. "I'll visit," she said softly. "All the time. I promise."

He stayed behind his ears. But he patted her gently on the shoulder with his trunk. **Tronk**, he said, and it sounded to Erica like *Thank you*.

The Second Chapter:
In which the Elephant earns a reputation

The next morning there was a gaggle of people on the front doorstep. Erica saw them from her bedroom window, and watched them argue about who should ring the bell and speak to her. "Well, if they have been sent by Uncle Jeff as well," said Erica, "that is tough. They aren't coming past the front door." And she went downstairs wearing the sternest face she could manage. (It was not bad. She had learnt it from a furious stuffed owl that Uncle Jeff kept in the living room.)

She opened the door. "Yes?"

The Gaggle looked shifty, and nudged each other, and ummed, which was not really an answer. At last one of them piped up: "We hear you've got an Elephant."

Erica wanted to say that she wasn't sure whether she had got an Elephant or an Elephant had got her, and that anyway they were about to un-get each other so it was all beside the point. But she thought that if she tried to talk about it she might get upset, and it really wasn't any of their business. So instead she just said, "Yes," and carried on looking like the Furious Owl.

This information made the Gaggle brave. "Can we see it?" asked several at once.

Erica opened her mouth to say no, because you can't invite strangers in to gawk at someone before they've even had breakfast. Then she remembered that there wasn't any breakfast, of either cornflakes or cabbage. She remembered the £30.42, which was all she had left in the world, and how upset the Elephant had been to learn that she couldn't afford to keep him. "Wait here," she ordered the Gaggle. "I'll see if he's awake."

She sped up the stairs and told the Elephant her idea, and he **TRONK**ed in delight so loudly it made her stagger a little.

Back down the stairs she went, patter-patter-patter.

"You may see him," she announced very grandly. "Three pounds entry, please."

The Gaggle didn't even grumble; they were so excited to see a Real Live Actual Elephant. Suddenly, Erica had doubled her money. They clattered upstairs and admired the Elephant, who had draped himself in curtains tugged off Uncle Jeff's window, to give the viewing a Sense of Occasion. He behaved beautifully, stealing their things with his trunk to make them shriek before handing them gently back, trumpeting tunes through his trunk, and altogether giving them a bargain for their three pounds.

When they had gone, Erica went to the shops and bought one large blackboard, one stick of chalk and all the cabbage she could carry. She brought it back to the Elephant, helped him get the curtains off his back (which proved to be a much more puzzling matter for him than getting them on), made a cup of tea and sat sipping it on the stairs while he munched cabbage in the hall.

"I think," she said, "that we have found an answer. If you don't mind doing it?"

TRONK, said the Elephant. It was a bit hard to understand because he had his mouth full, but it sounded like he meant *Of course I don't.*

"I don't suppose you can do rides, with

your bad knee?" she asked.

He stopped chewing and looked her in the eye. He was cross, and she remembered that he didn't like her to worry about his knee. With great dignity he started chewing again, cabbage hanging out of his mouth, and ignored the question. So she took the hint, and wrote on her blackboard:

Visit the amazing Elephant!
Viewing – £3
Rides – £6

And she drew a picture of the Elephant

at the bottom, which delighted him. She propped the board against the wall of the house. It was a strange sight, sitting next to the boring geraniums in window boxes. Nothing else about the house suggested that there might be a girl living by herself with an elephant.

Then they waited.

And waited.

They waited some more, but now with less enthusiasm. The Elephant's stomach started to grumble, reminding Erica that she had only given him a fraction of the cabbage he needed.

Eventually the living room grew darker as day turned to dusk. Erica and the Elephant did not meet each other's eyes.

It seemed they had been wrong. No one was interested in seeing a girl and her hungry Elephant.

Neither of them wanted to be the first to say "Shall we go to bed?", so they stayed up as the sky outside grew black and the town grew quiet. The Elephant had his back against the radiator, and Erica had her back against the Elephant. When his hungry stomach rumbled she felt the rumbling in her bones, and even though she was a very practical girl, it was such a sad sound that she let out a little sob.

They slept late the next morning, and when they eventually woke up, it was to the sound of an impatient Gaggle banging on the front door. Erica looked out of her window and squealed in surprise and delight. The queue stretched all the way down the street!

They raced into action, Erica changing from pyjamas into her smartest clothes and finding a bucket for the money, the Elephant insisting on putting on the curtains again and admiring himself in the mirror. "We'll have to have them ten at a time!" Erica called to him as she hunted for her hairbrush. "We can do it in the garden, since it's a dry day, and then you can give rides. In very small circles. Give everyone, say, ten turns of the garden. Try not to trample the flowerbeds if you can help it." She was pattering down the stairs now. "Are you ready? Right, you go outside and I'll open the door!"

So the Elephant trotted unsteadily off to the back door, the curtain trailing behind him, while Erica ran to the front door and opened it at last. They began.

Word had taken time to spread, but now that it had, there was no end to the queue. People kept coming. Erica had to keep emptying out her bucket when the change was getting too heavy. There were tourists and locals, young and old, bold and timid. One boy was so afraid of the Elephant that

he climbed the apple tree and watched in awe from up there.

At lunchtime, business people in suits came with their sandwiches and coffees, and the Elephant unknotted and knotted their ties with his trunk (which was so impressive that even Erica clapped), and ruffled their hair, and stole their mobile phones when they tried to make Important Calls.

Erica served everyone lemonade and organized the rides. The Elephant was pleased as punch to be giving rides again. He limped a little, but no one seemed to mind.

When they were dealing with the last ten people of the day, Miss Pritchett from Next Door appeared over the fence. She was a very small elderly lady, and to see over the fence she had to stand on a box. One minute she wasn't there, and the next minute she popped up, just high enough for you to see her tiny frowning face. She had always seemed to Erica like a horrible jack-in-the-box, springing up over the fence without warning to tell Uncle Jeff off about something or ask Erica nosy questions.

"Good afternoon, Miss Pritchett," said Erica.

"Good afternoon," said Miss Pritchett, as if it wasn't. "Where on earth did you get that Elephant?"

"Uncle Jeff sent him," said Erica, although what she wanted to say was, *Where on earth did you get that nose of yours, always in other people's business?*

Miss Pritchett's face got even smaller and crosser at the mention of Uncle Jeff. "Well, don't parade it around! Someone might call the council. Or the police!"

You mean you *might call the police*, thought Erica. But she just said, "We'll try not to disturb anyone."

"It doesn't matter whether you *disturb*

people," said Miss Pritchett. "People have a habit of being disturbed by all sorts of silly things. The point is that you really shouldn't have an Elephant in your house at all."

Erica pulled herself up as tall as she could. "I'm afraid it is *his* house too now," she said, "so he will be staying." And before Miss Pritchett could rant at her any more, she hurried off to round up the chattering visitors and see them out of the garden, ignoring the muttering and grumbling that was still drifting over the fence.

When she had shut the back door, she could no longer hear Miss Pritchett, but it was not so easy to shut out the thought that she might report them both. Being a very practical girl, Erica came up with a plan. "Tomorrow," she said to the Elephant, "we will go down to the beach, and then you can give rides by the sea. Miss Pritchett can't complain about that, and we'll get more business there anyway."

And so they settled into a happy routine. They would set off to the beach bright and early, before Miss Pritchett had begun twitching open her curtains. The Elephant would entertain everyone until five o'clock, performing clever tricks and giving rides, with plenty of breaks for cabbage (for him) and ice cream (for Erica). He would sway along by the edge of the sea with delighted humans on his back, while cameras clicked and seagulls cawed in surprise. Then the two of them would go home via the corner shop, buying Erica dinner (the Elephant's cabbage had to be ordered in bulk online).

There was always something left in their bucket to save up for the future. "When we have enough," Erica would promise, "we'll redo Uncle Jeff's room so that it feels like a proper home for you. You can choose some paint, and we'll get you a big pile of bedding, and do something to fix the bits of the wall you've broken."

The Elephant would just **TRONK** in

a pleased sort of way, because he wasn't sure how to explain that it already felt like a proper home, and also because he wasn't *quite* sure what paint was.

Erica had never been happier. It had been strange without Uncle Jeff these last two years, living in an empty house, and as Uncle Jeff had never thought of sending her to school, she didn't know any other children. With the Elephant, the house was suddenly gloriously full, and she spent her evenings curled up against his side in the last free inch of the living room.

What's more, she was meeting new people all day. There was always someone who would buy an ice cream and sit next to her for a while to chat while the Elephant gave rides. Some of them came back more than once, so she started to get to know them. There were the identical twins, who were staying with their aunt during their school holidays, and a young woman who was writing a novel about the Spanish Armada, and an elderly couple who liked to feed the seagulls and disagree with each other.

Her favourite was an enormously tall and spindly man called Oliver Drew, who had round glasses and curly hair that stuck up at strange angles. He knew everything there was to know about animals in general, and elephants in particular.

"Did you know they can make noises that are much too deep for us humans to

hear? It's a sort of rumble," he told her one day, as they licked their ice creams. "The other elephants can hear it though, and at huge distances. They can call each other from six miles away on a still day."

"*Six miles?*" said Erica. "That's crazy!"

"It's important! Elephants are very social. They need their herd to survive. They feel each others' vibrations with their trunk and feet as well as their ears," Oliver explained. "Always watch an elephant's ears. If they are flapping, the elephant is either happy or angry."

Oliver was always giving her tips like this, as if the Elephant's messages were a difficult puzzle you could solve by knowing the right clues. Erica was too polite to tell him that she could always tell what the Elephant meant without using this kind of trick. But Oliver was only trying to help, and was excellent company, and really loved the Elephant. He loved the story of his arrival on her doorstep, and their strange life together. When she told him how the Elephant had wrecked Uncle Jeff's room, he laughed so hard that he shook his ice cream everywhere.

"You'll have to come and see it for yourself some time," said Erica, "before we patch it all up."

He agreed, and they arranged that he would come over for tea the next week, and swapped telephone numbers and addresses. So now Erica had *two* friends, not to mention a lot of ice cream.

Even Miss Pritchett couldn't spoil Erica's mood when they met her on the way home that day. She was trimming the hedge in front of her house, snipping each unwanted twig with a smart click and tossing it aside. As she saw the pair approach, she stopped snipping at twigs and started snapping at them instead. "Erica," she yapped, "have you been parading that Elephant around again?"

"Good evening, Miss Pritchett," said Erica politely. "He's been parading himself, really."

"Never mind your smart-alec talk. He should be in the house. Don't you know the risks?"

Yes, thought Erica, *there's a risk someone might have some fun instead of endlessly snipping their hedges and nagging.* But she said, "We'll be careful, Miss Pritchett," as she unlocked the front door. The Elephant nodded his head in agreement so enthusiastically that his ears flapped around and knocked a passing wren out of the air, which didn't exactly reassure Miss Pritchett.

"Mind you do! You're asking for trouble!" she called out, as the door shut behind them.

Silly woman, thought Erica. But although Erica was a very practical girl, she was not always wise. However silly people might seem to you, it can be unwise to ignore them.

The Third Chapter:
In which the problems really begin

The next day, Erica and the Elephant were taking a day off. She had gently suggested that he might like to try using the bath, so he was upstairs finding out about taps, while she read a book in the living room. Suddenly, there were three sharp raps on the door. TAT-TAT-TAT: LET-ME-IN.

Erica opened it to find a stout woman on the doorstep, dressed entirely in polka dots – a black-and-white polka-dot skirt, a blue-and-pink polka-dot blouse, and red-and-white polka-dot shoes. She had topped it off with a knitted polka-dot hat.

"Hello, dear," she said. "Can I come in?"

By the time she had finished the sentence she was already inside, so there didn't seem to be a lot of point in saying no.

"My name is Amy Avis, and I'm here to talk about

something very important. Are your mummy and daddy home?"

Erica explained that she lived by herself. An almighty CRASH came from the bathroom upstairs, so she added, "With the Elephant."

Amy Avis looked very shocked and produced a polka-dot notebook to write this down in. *Although*, thought Erica, *I don't see why she's bothering. "No parents, one elephant" is easy to remember.*

But Amy Avis wrote it down anyway, and then started trotting uninvited through the downstairs of the house, tutting and writing more things down. Erica was suddenly very aware how untidy the house was. The trouble with the Elephant was that he did tend to leave a mess.

"What was it you wanted to talk about, Mrs Avis?" asked Erica, when it began to seem as if the trotting and tutting would go on for ever.

Amy Avis turned her gaze on Erica as if she was slightly surprised to find that she could talk. "Ah. Yes," she said. "Have a seat, dear."

This muddled Erica, who had been about to offer Mrs Avis a seat to make her stop the unsettling trotting. It is odd to be offered your own kitchen chair by your guest. But there didn't seem to be anything else to do but sit down. Amy Avis, meanwhile, started looking out of the window and tutting at the garden, so Erica said, "Well?" quite sharply to distract her from the mess out there.

"I have come about your Elephant," said Amy Avis.

Erica's gut went wobbly with nerves at that, because she was pretty sure that someone who wore that many polka dots and tutted at other people's houses hadn't come to see an elephant for fun.

"Now, don't be worried, dear. You're not in any trouble. But you can't keep an elephant without a Licence, you know." And she giggled, as if Erica had done something very silly and quite funny. "Goodness me, no! It's all right though, we can take care of it for you. I'm from the

Department of Exotic Animals. I've been sent with a Notice of Elephant Extraction, and the Department will send a van round for the animal this afternoon. So you won't have to worry about looking after that great big Elephant any more!" Amy fished in her polka-dot handbag. "Here's your Notice. And here's a toffee." She put both of these on the table.

Now, the worst way to tell someone bad news is to pretend that it is good news and ignore how horrible they are feeling. You won't fool them, and it makes them feel like they are screaming and no one can hear them. Erica ignored the toffee. She opened her mouth to say something very rude, when she suddenly remembered:

"I *do* have a Licence!"

Amy Avis's smile vanished. "Now, dear, you mustn't—" she began. But Erica had already jumped up from her chair and sped to the living room, where she pulled open her Important Papers drawer to find the bit of paper saying she had a Right to the Elephant.

She took this triumphantly to Amy Avis, who pulled a pair of glasses from the enormous handbag, perched them on the end of her nose and read the paper at arm's length. "Oh no, dear," she said, giggling again. "No, no. This isn't a Licence. It's just proof of sale. You have a Right to the Elephant as far as the owner was concerned. But you need a Licence from the British Government to say you can keep it."

Erica wished she wouldn't refer to the Elephant as "it". She wished Uncle Jeff had thought to check the law before merrily sending her an elephant. She wished she

could rewind time five minutes and not open the door, keeping Amy Avis outside and the lovely lazy day inside.

Amy Avis rambled on. "Now, you're not to worry, dear. We'll take him to a zoo, where he'll be very happy. You're not in any trouble." She seemed certain that the most upsetting thing that could happen was Being in Trouble.

"What happens if I don't let you take him?" asked Erica.

Amy Avis's mouth fell open into a startled "O", like another silly polka dot. "Well, dear," she said, a little less kindly, "we would have to take him anyway. And you really shouldn't try that, because then you *will* be in very serious trouble."

"What happens if *he* won't let you take him?"

She giggled her silly giggle. "Well, I really can't see why there would be any trouble on that front. But if it was aggressive, we would just have to sedate it." Erica thought she couldn't hate anyone more than Amy Avis at that moment. "I hope it *isn't* aggressive. You should tell us if it is, dear. The caller who spoke to us about it was very worried." And then Erica hated Miss Pritchett most of all.

While Amy Avis gave a lecture about how dangerous elephants were, Erica stopped listening and started forming a Plan. She knew, with sudden certainty, that she was not willing to give up the

Elephant. It would break his heart, and she would have to go back to living in a silent house with no more friendly evenings together or busy days at the beach. They would have to run away. She didn't know where they would run to, but the main thing was to run as far as they could, and then find somewhere to lie low. She did her best to look meek and sorry while she thought through the possible routes.

After an eternity of giggling and saying "dear" and occasionally tutting, Amy Avis finally left, pausing on her way out to write in her notebook about the broken door frame. Erica slammed the door shut, but not fast enough to block out the chirpy sound of "See you this afternoon, dear!".

She raced upstairs to the Elephant. He was in the bathroom, where he had been spraying himself — and the floor — with water from a full bathtub. He was lying on his side, and it seemed to Erica that he looked a paler shade of grey than usual. He said a very quiet **Tronk**.

"No, you are NOT fine," replied Erica. "Don't try and be noble. What happened?"

The Elephant waved his trunk sadly at the water, and then at his knee, breathing out another unhappy **TROOOOOOONK**.

"You slipped?" guessed Erica. "Has it hurt your bad knee?"

He **TRONK**ed in a resigned sort of way.

"Can you walk?" she asked.

The Elephant tried to stand, wobbled, turned a little paler and sank back down again.

Erica looked at him in dismay. Even if you are the most practical girl in the world, getting an elephant out of town at speed when it cannot walk is a challenge. She knelt down and hugged the Elephant very hard, and told him as kindly as she could what had just happened. The Elephant flapped his ears angrily and made another bid to stand. This time he staggered as far as the door before falling again.

Erica couldn't think what to do or who to turn to – *Which just shows*, she thought,

that the Elephant is the only friend I've got.
She remembered what Oliver had told her about elephants needing their herd to survive. *Humans need herds too*, she thought.

Then – "Oh!" she said. "Oliver!"

TRONK, said the Elephant, which didn't seem to mean anything much except *Ow*.

Erica stroked his side. "Hold on," she said. "I'm going to call for help. We'll be OK."

She stepped carefully over his head and pattered down to the kitchen, fishing Oliver's number out of her pocket as she ran. She was so hasty dialling the number that she got it wrong and panted, "Help, they're going to take the Elephant!" to the owner of a fish-and-chip shop, which confused them both. She dialled more carefully, crossed her fingers, and waited. After five rings, Oliver's voice cut in. "Oliver Drew speaking."

"Oliver! They're going to take the Elephant!"

"Erica? Is that you?"

"Yes! She said I have to have a Licence and she tried to give me toffee!" Erica was so happy to hear Oliver and so frantic that she said everything all at once in the wrong order, and he had to make her start again and tell him slowly and carefully.

When she had finished, Oliver was

silent for a few seconds. "What should I do, Oliver? Can you help?"

"I'm trying to think of a way, Erica," he said. "I'm not in town right now." She groaned at that. "But don't panic. You did the right thing to call me. Now, whatever you do, don't try and leave with the Elephant before his knee has healed. I know something that might help him heal faster — but if it doesn't work in time, I want you to promise me you won't leave. If you leave while it's still bad, it will only get worse and you won't get far enough. And if they think you've hurt him, you'll never get him back. Do you understand, Erica? Promise me you won't leave until his knee is better?"

Erica promised, and wrote down all the ingredients Oliver listed for a special medicine for animal joints. He was so kind and calm that when he finally had to go, and she heard the click of his phone hanging up, she felt even lonelier than before. Part of her wanted to give in there and then. But she had to make the medicine, and some of the ingredients weren't in the house, so she put on her sandals to go in to town and Get On With Things. If you are in a difficult situation, Getting On With Things is always a good choice.

Buying the ingredients took her a while, as some were very unusual, and she had to trail around town trying to find them (guava juice certainly wasn't in the supermarket – and she didn't even know what star anise *was*). When she had them all, she had to boil the mixture and then let it simmer for an hour. It all seemed unbearably slow. While it simmered she went to sit with the Elephant, who curled his trunk around her, and they told each other about how it would be all right. Neither of them sounded very sure.

When the medicine was finally ready, she fed it to the Elephant, and found an old tartan scarf of Uncle Jeff's to bandage up his knee in the vague hope that this would help too.

It seemed to her that an hour later he looked a bit less pale, although he still couldn't stand. After two hours he tried to insist that he could, but he couldn't hide how much it hurt, and she made him sit down again. She could just imagine Amy Avis tutting and writing in her notebook that she had hurt the Elephant.

Nobody else ever seemed to realize that the Elephant did things for himself.

It was clear that the Elephant wasn't going to be ready to leave that day. After lunch he insisted he was feeling better, and trod gingerly down the stairs, leaning against the banister and cracking it in places as he went. But by the time he got to the bottom he was worn out. It was no good. The medicine wasn't working fast enough.

Erica kept looking nervously out of the window for the van. Every car made her jump. She didn't see the van, but what she *did* see, at about half past three, was Miss Pritchett coming back from town. Erica knew that shouting at Miss Pritchett wasn't going to help, but she was very upset, and even very practical people have tantrums every now and then. So she ran outside and began shouting as loudly as her small human lungs could manage.

"Erica," said Miss Pritchett, and when that didn't stop the shouting, she said, "Erica!" and then, "ERICA!"

This last one was so forceful for such a tiny lady that Erica stopped in sheer surprise. "Are you trying to tell me," said Miss Pritchett, "that someone has reported that Elephant of yours?"

Erica carried on feeling very cross, but just a little less certain. "You mean that *you* have reported him." She paused. "Haven't you?"

"No," said Miss Pritchett. "Although I

can't say I'm surprised that someone has, with you showing him off for all the world to see. Have you sent him away somewhere sensible?"

Erica didn't know what to think, so she just said, "I can't. He's hurt his knee."

"Oh dear," said Miss Pritchett, and she folded her face up in a slightly different way, which looked a little less cross and a little more worried. "That *is* a problem. What a pair of idiots. Well, I suppose you'd better hide him in my house then. Can he get that far?"

Erica looked hard at Miss Pritchett, and tried to guess what she was up to. Why would she want to get the Elephant into her house? Hadn't she already won? What difference did it make now? Unless, of course, she was telling the truth. The old lady was grumpy and sharp-tongued and nosy, but she didn't seem like a liar.

Miss Pritchett must have guessed her thoughts. "Come *on*, Erica" she said. "Look at it this way: if I'm lying and I turn him in, you're no worse off than you were before. And if I'm not lying, then I might be able to help." And no matter which way Erica thought about this, it still seemed to be true.

So, three minutes later, Erica and the Elephant were going into Miss Pritchett's by the back door (to avoid being seen), not knowing what to think but just about daring to hope.

The Fourth Chapter:
In which hiding an Elephant proves to be tricky

Erica had never tried to imagine the inside of Miss Pritchett's house. If she had, she would not have come up with this.

The whole place was full of ants.

Wherever Erica looked, there were glass containers full of soil: on shelves lining the walls, on every flat surface, even hanging like wind chimes from the ceiling. Each one was laced all over with tunnels, and up and down the tunnels scurried the ants. There were black ants and red ants; some as big as your thumb and some almost too small to see; quick ants and slow ants; ants in lines and clumps and on lone missions. Erica couldn't take her eyes off them. Everywhere you looked, a tiny six-legged someone was doing something with an air of Great Importance.

Miss Pritchett smiled a tiny smile. "You and your uncle aren't the only ones keen on exotic animals. I have more species of ant here than any other collector in England," she said proudly. "Nobody needs a Licence for ants, Erica, and I highly recommend them. Wonderful fellows. Tiny, but stronger than your elephant relative to their size — they can lift things that weigh five thousand times more than their own body."

The Elephant, kneeling slightly to rest his bad leg, considered the nearest box. His trunk was firmly curled inwards. He looked like he wouldn't want to keep ants even if they could juggle and dance the Macarena. "Tea?" said Miss Pritchett.

Erica was still hunting for the catch, but she couldn't see a catch to tea, so she just said yes. And then, because sometimes it is best to tackle things head on, she said, "Miss Pritchett, why are you helping us when you hate the Elephant so much?"

Miss Pritchett's face unfolded into a stretched-out sheet of surprise. "What on earth makes you think I hate him?"

Erica was so pleased that she had said "him" and not "it" that she suddenly felt wrong-footed. "Um," she said. "Well, because," she added. "Because of the – er, um," she explained. And Miss Pritchett just kept looking at her, frowning, because she wasn't making a lot of sense. So at last she said, "Because you were always so cross with us."

"I was cross with you for parading him around. Someone was bound to report you. If *I* wanted to report you, I would have called the police the day he arrived." She poured boiling water into the teapot. "It's no problem to me if you want to keep an Elephant. I've heard they're very

good company. Lord knows, he must be better than that uncle of yours. I'll be giving him a piece of my mind when he gets back – he *promised* me this would just be a short trip."

Erica began to feel very foolish. It was true that Miss Pritchett was prickly and a little rude. But it was clear that Erica hadn't been listening to her properly – and not just about the Elephant. It dawned on her that all that nosy muttering over the fence at Uncle Jeff had probably been Miss Pritchett's way of looking out for her. "Oh," she said. "I misunderstood."

"Don't look so much like a slapped fish," said Miss Pritchett. "Lord knows, I don't speak poetry. You wouldn't be the first person to think I'm a nasty old fool." Erica felt like she should say sorry, but Miss Pritchett seemed perfectly cheerful about it. She brought the teapot over and sat down across the table from Erica, looking at her without smiling, but not unkindly. "It's one of the hazards of being human, Erica. Take ants. They're deaf, and some species are blind. They tell each other what's going on with chemical signals – one for danger, one for food, and what have you. Simple. Meanwhile we tie ourselves in knots trying to understand each other, and half the time we get it wrong." She poured the tea and Erica sipped hers, suddenly feeling very tired. The Elephant was staying very still, concentrating on not smashing any glass boxes, and eyeing the ants suspiciously.

"Now," said Miss Pritchett – and it was the sort of "now" that made Erica put down her tea and the Elephant straighten his trunk importantly – "when are these meddlers coming?"

"Any time this afternoon."

"Right, then we've no time to lose. You," she said to the Elephant, "need to leave prints through your garden and smash up the back fence, then get inside my bathroom. That's the only room where they can't spot you through a window. You" – she turned back to Erica – "need to go next door and tell them he's run away."

"Will they believe me?" asked Erica.

"Oh, I doubt it," she replied. "But as long as they can't find the Elephant, there won't be very much they can do about it. You might have to stay here a few days, you know," she warned the Elephant, "and then we will come up with something else."

Soon two humans and one elephant were scuttling about as busily as the worker ants. The Elephant, slowly and a little painfully, smashed his way out of the garden. Erica was delighted to see that he could already walk for longer before taking a rest, and she thanked heaven for Oliver and his medicine. Miss Pritchett tidied up the signs that an elephant had

been in the kitchen while Erica ran to
the shops for cabbage supplies.

The Elephant made himself as small
as he could in Miss Pritchett's bathroom.

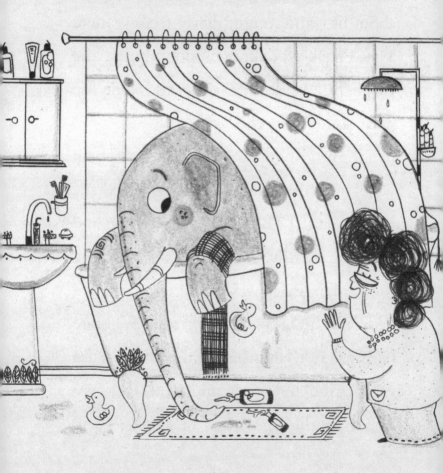

"You mustn't move at all," Miss Pritchett warned him. "These houses are terraced. I could always hear every move you made through that wall."

So he curled up tightly and waited. Miss Pritchett went back downstairs, and waited. Next door, Erica waited.

At last, a black van approached. On the side were a logo and the words:

Department of Exotic Animals and Hats

This was odd, but Erica didn't have time to wonder what it might mean, because Amy Avis and two balding men were already walking to her door and TAT-

TAT-TATing. *LET-ME-IN*.

She did her best to look sorry when she opened the door. Amy Avis sailed inside with a breezy "Hello, dear", and was followed silently by the two men, who wore shirts with the same logo that was stamped on the van. She took a deep breath. "I'm very sorry, Mrs Avis. It's – I – the Elephant has run away." And it seemed like such a mad, obvious lie that Erica almost *did* feel sorry as she said it, so it came out of her mouth in the right sort of quivering way.

Amy Avis looked at Erica. Both of the men looked at Erica. Erica tried very hard to look like someone who didn't know where their Elephant was. She almost wished that Amy Avis would tut, to break the silence. Instead, she said, "Erica. You shouldn't tell lies. We will still take it away, and you will be in trouble too."

"Really, he has!" said Erica. "Search the house!"

So they did. It didn't take them long, because the house was not large, but they were at a loss for what else to do so they searched it three times. Amy Avis trotted in front and the two men mooched behind, opening things here and there as if they half expected the Elephant to be in a drawer. They put their ears to the floorboards and tapped the walls to find hollow bits, and looked under beds.

At last, with the air of one having made a great discovery, Amy Avis announced, "It appears that the Elephant is not in the house." No one disagreed. "We will have to search the town. Erica, this was *very* careless of you."

The three then began a furious muttering among themselves to decide on their next move. When they had muttered their way to a decision, Amy Avis nodded to Erica. "Some questions in the living room, please."

The questions were endless. *When did you last see it? Where does it like to go? Has it any friends among the local wildlife? Does it fit on a bus?* On and on. Erica made up answers at random, while inside, her heart applauded with a pounding clap-clap-clap. It looked like this was going to work.

"Has the animal, to your knowledge, ever learned to ride a bicycle," asked Man Number One, "or any other form of—" And then he was interrupted by something that is hard to write down, but went a bit like this: **AaaahTROSHnshk**.

All four humans froze. Erica's heart stopped applauding.

AaaahTRRRROSHnshk. There it was again. And again. Three unexplained **aahTROSHnshks**. There was a nasty silence in the living room.

"My next-door neighbour plays the trombone," Erica heard herself saying. **AaahTROSHnshk** went the Noise, and she added, "Very badly."

"That," said Man Number Two, "is not a trombone."

Without a word, the three all rose and made their way to the front door, and Erica followed. Her mouth carried on trying to fix things, but without any help from her brain, which seemed to be taking a break. "Oh, please, you mustn't disturb her. She has to play a fanfare for the Queen tomorrow." A most un-royal **aahTROSHnshk** cut her off.

Amy Avis adjusted her polka-dot hat and gave her smart TAT-TAT-TAT on Miss Pritchett's door. After a short pause the old lady opened it. She did an excellent job of looking elephantless and cross.

"Yes?" she snapped.

"Madam," said Amy Avis. "We believe you have an Elephant in your house."

"Well, I never heard the like!" said Miss Pritchett, blocking the doorway.

Again the awful Noise blasted out. **AaahTROSHnshk**.

"I am in the middle of an important chemistry experiment," said Miss Pritchett. "Please excuse the explosions."

Amy Avis was not fooled. "How nice," she replied, "that you find time for science, when you have a royal fanfare to prepare for." Miss Pritchett's eyes flickered very briefly to Erica. "May we come in?"

Miss Pritchett began to close the door, saying that the experiment needed

Important Stirring. But Man Number One had already put his foot in the way, and Man Number Two gave the door a shove, and before anyone could stop her, Amy Avis was trotting inside.

And up the stairs, towards the bathroom...

The Fifth Chapter:
In which the truth comes out

It is widely believed that elephants are afraid of mice. This is nonsense. Ants, however, are a different matter.

Some types of ant live in trees, and they have to battle with elephants who try to eat their houses. Battling an elephant is easier said than done when you are smaller than a raisin. So the ants are cunning: they send soldier ants to crawl up the elephants' trunks and tickle them from the inside. This is not pleasant. The result is a lot of startled sneezing from the elephant in question, which sounds – as you have no doubt guessed – a bit like this: **aahTROSHnshk**.

Miss Pritchett said it was her fault for leaving the lid off one of the boxes. But the Elephant could not be persuaded to blame anyone but himself. For the whole journey in the van, he stayed firmly hidden behind his ears, which had blushed a greyish sort of pink. Miss Pritchett prattled away, raining curses on Amy Avis and the Department of Exotic Animals and Hats and the government and even the Queen, while Erica sat in tense silence. No one had told them where they were going.

They were going, it turned out, to the police station. Amy Avis was hopping mad that Erica had made her trot around the house so foolishly, and was now on the war path. She wanted the two humans charged with housing an elephant, and the Elephant charged with improper use of a bathroom.

The Officer on duty at the police station tugged nervously at his moustache. "I am not sure we can charge an elephant, ma'am," he said.

Amy Avis tutted wildly. "Of course you can! I demand to see your superior! I demand a lawyer! I demand action!"

This was too many demands for the Officer to cope with. He went to ask a more important Officer, and she made some phone calls and reported that no one else had any clue what to do about an elephant either, but told him he had to do *something*. So he returned to them and did his best to sound firm. "Ladies," he said, "there has certainly been a breach of the law here, insomuch as there is, as it were, an Elephant, and the Elephant in question is, so to speak, without a Licence. However, we are − ahem − unclear as to the legal process in such a case. We shall therefore accommodate the suspected − er, well, the Elephant and its friends − in temporary custody until we have the information to proceed."

"By which you mean," said Miss Pritchett, "that you are just going to lock us up until you get your act together?"

The Officer said a loud "Ahem", and quickly carried on, addressing Amy Avis. "Your contact at the zoo has been called. He will stop by this evening to deal with the paperwork and remove the animal in the morning."

Amy Avis looked like she was still hoping for a more immediate and terrible punishment, but as she had more or less won, she settled for some mild tutting. Miss Pritchett grumbled all the way to their cell, but no one was listening any more. With a relieved BANG, the Officer shut the door on the sorry trio, and marched quickly away. There was a short silence.

"Elephant?" said Erica. Silence. "I'm sorry I got us in to this mess." A drop more silence, and then the Elephant **Tronk**ed very slightly. Erica couldn't make out what he meant, but it seemed

to be a comforting sort of **TRONK**. So she left it there. Although none of them spoke, their thoughts seemed to fill the cell. There was a single wooden bench, so Erica and Miss Pritchett curled up there, while the Elephant took up most of the rest of the remaining space. A clock on the wall tutted, like a tightly wound Amy Avis.

After an hour or so, they heard the tap-tap of feet coming down the corridor, and with a rattle and click, the Officer let a visitor into their cell. A visitor with curling hair that stuck out in all directions at once, and a long and spindly body. Erica leaped off the bench. "Oliver!" she cried.

Oliver didn't smile. "Erica," he said, "I

told you not to try and run away."

She deflated very slightly. "We didn't, Oliver. We hid him. He hardly had to do any walking at all. I've been giving him the medicine, just like you said."

"You're in a lot of trouble now, Erica. That was stupid." All the warmth had gone out of Oliver's voice. He spoke *at* Erica rather than *to* her, as if she was a bad TV programme or a shrill and unwelcome alarm clock. He folded up his spidery limbs to crouch down next to the Elephant and peered at his bad leg. "His walk is getting better, I assume?"

"Yes, I think so," said Erica, and she meant to say "Thanks to you", but something about the way Oliver was looking at the Elephant stopped her. Instead, a very uncomfortable silence crept in and filled the space where her sentence should have been. Oliver had untied the scarf around the Elephant's knee, and was now feeling the knee carefully, testing the damage with expert hands. At length he unfolded upwards, his shadow snaking out and falling over the Elephant as he stood.

"Not too much damage. He's still a very fine elephant indeed. I don't suppose that uncle of yours had any idea what a beauty he'd found." He was smiling, but only with his mouth. "I owe him a thank you."

Erica opened her mouth and shut it again, which was one of her less useful decisions. Happily, Miss Pritchett had plenty to say. Her face was folded up more tightly than Erica had ever seen it. "Who," she barked, "are you, young man?" Oliver said he was Oliver Drew, and Miss Pritchett clicked her tongue. "Your name is beside the point. I'm not writing a phone book. I mean, what is your business here?"

He seemed to find her amusing. "Yes, ma'am. I am the manager of Seabreeze Zoo, and I am here to check that my newest elephant is in good health before I collect him tomorrow. "

So *that* was why Oliver knew all about animals. But Erica still couldn't understand why he was helping Amy Avis. There had to be some mistake. "Why are you agreeing to take him?" she said. "You know he's happy with me!"

Oliver looked bored again. "Do keep up, Erica. It was me who reported you. The whole *point* was to take the Elephant. With the tricks this creature can do, the zoo will have people coming from miles around." Erica gaped at him. The Elephant did too, but it was hard to tell under his trunk. "Come ON. You show me a wonderful elephant, and then tell me there's no adult at home. And then you tell me where you live, and the next day there's a knock on your door. Did you really not add it all up?"

"Did the medicine – did it make him worse?"

"Of course not. I want him in good health. It doesn't do anything at all. The 'ingredients' were my shopping list." He

said all this as if it was terribly dull. Erica tried very hard not to cry. "A word of advice, Erica. Make some friends your own size. Elephants are complicated. It takes expertise to look after one." And without waiting for her to respond Oliver ducked out of the cell, letting the door clang shut behind him.

"Well, he was a *horrid* man," said Miss Pritchett, in case anybody wasn't sure.

"He's wrong," said Erica. "Elephants aren't complicated at all. It's *people* I can't seem to get the hang of." And now she did cry, just a bit. Neither Miss Pritchett nor the Elephant spoke, but they sat on either side of her on the floor, one arm and one trunk around her shoulders. In the end it was Erica who broke the silence. She was thinking how glad she was to have her friends there with her, and this made her wonder. . . "Elephant," she said, "do you miss your herd?"

TRONK. *Yes.*

"I'm sorry I never thought to ask about them." The Elephant sighed, ruffling Erica's hair. "Do you know about elephant herds, Miss Pritchett? They look out for each other. They can hear each other from up to six miles away on a still day." And this almost started Erica crying again, remembering how she had called on Oliver for help.

"*Six miles?*" said Miss Pritchett.

"I know, it's amazing. The noise is too

low for humans to hear. A sort of rumbling."

"ERICA!" yelled Miss Pritchett, leaping up. "Don't you know what you've said? Don't you see what this means? Don't just sit there moping, girl! This is brilliant!"

"What is brilliant?"

"The zoo," said Miss Pritchett, scrunching her face into an enormous smile, "is about *five miles away*."

"Oh!" said Erica. Then, after thinking about it some more, she added, "So?"

Miss Pritchett's wrinkles had rearranged themselves into a wicked grin. "I think," she said, "we should call for a little help. Elephant, can you pass on a message to an elephant five miles away?" The Elephant nodded, ears flapping. "Then how about this. . ." And she told them her plan. The Elephant laughed and laughed. Erica was used to his laugh, but it was a very strange sound, and it seriously alarmed the man in the cell next door. (Perhaps you have never heard an elephant laugh? It sounds a bit like this: **aaahTROOhoohooHOOO**. To get the full effect, you need to sing it through a megaphone in your best Operatic Voice – otherwise it will just sound silly.)

Erica did not feel like laughing. The plan was too mad to work. "We will *never* pull that off!" she said.

"Now, Erica," said Miss Pritchett, "you have to think big, if you want to do something as ridiculously big as keeping an elephant." Erica had never seen Miss Pritchett look so pleased.

"Won't they just send the Elephant to another zoo?"

Miss Pritchett cackled. "Not if you scare them off, Erica..." And she told them the rest of her plan, and they all laughed until their sides hurt.

When they had calmed down, the Elephant shut his eyes and began his deep rumbling, feeling for an answer in his ears and trunk and feet. They waited tensely. What if the zoo was too far away after all?

But the Elephant's ears twitched, and then his trunk waggled in a pleased sort of way, and he gave them a happy **TRONK**. The elephants at the zoo had the message, and now Erica and Miss Pritchett had to send out their own. Both asked to call their families, and were given five minutes each with the telephone. No one knew that neither of them had any family to call.

The Sixth Chapter:
In which a whopping lie is told

When Oliver, Amy Avis and the Officer arrived, Erica was sitting perfectly still in the middle of the cell, her eyes shut, both arms raised. Her hair had been twirled and tugged by the Elephant until it stood out in a mane around her head, and she had strange shadowy marks on her face, which had been drawn with Miss Pritchett's eye shadow. Around her, some leaves brought for the Elephant had been arranged in a circle, and Miss Pritchett and the Elephant sat outside the circle, watching Erica.

The Officer coughed slightly. Amy

Avis tutted and Oliver smiled his mouth-only smile. Erica opened one eye. "Good morning," she said politely.

Only the Officer said "Good morning" back, and when he saw the way the other two were looking at her, he tried to turn it into a stern sort of coughing noise.

Erica's heart was beating very fast. She shut the open eye. "Oliver Drew. If you take this Elephant today, your zoo will suffer."

Oliver looked at her like she was mad. Amy Avis looked at her like she was mad. The Officer looked at his shoes and wished very hard that he had nice, normal criminals to deal with, instead of lunatics with an Elephant.

"Oh, really, Erica?" said Oliver. "And why is that?"

"I have placed a curse on it," she said. She tried not to blush in the awkward silence that followed.

"I see," said Oliver. "Well, that sounds rather unlikely. I think I'll take my chances. Shall we go?"

The Officer didn't need telling twice, and flung open the door with a CLANG, hurrying outside. The others followed, Amy Avis making notes about Erica as she went, while Erica chanted under her breath and walked slowly behind them. The Elephant brought up the rear. They all piled into the black van, and with a thrum from the engine they were off.

Erica found it very hard not to laugh at the oddball collection speeding along the motorway – a polka-dot-covered fusspot, an unsmiling snake of a man, the Officer (who by now had nearly tugged his moustache right off), a tiny old woman, and an Elephant – and she, Erica, sitting in the middle of the van and chanting. Outside, ordinary cars hummed past on their way to ordinary sensible things. In that moment, she decided she was rather glad an Elephant had arrived on her doorstep and caused her all this trouble.

When they got out of the van, it was raining very slightly. A bright red SEABREEZE ZOO sign swung backwards and forwards in the car park, looking sorry about its grey home. It was quiet. A little too quiet. No animals growling or whistling or trumpeting, and no humans queuing at the gates. Just the creaking of the sign.

"Well, let's get this animal a home!" said Amy Avis brightly, and she click-clacked towards the gate. The others followed, but Oliver had stopped smiling, and seemed to have coiled inwards a little – a snake on the defence. As they walked, a teenager in a red SEABREEZE ZOO T-shirt came running out to meet him. Her badge said: **SANDRA. HOW CAN I HELP YOU TODAY?**

"Mr Drew," she said, "we've had to send everyone home. There's – there's something wrong with the animals."

"What on earth do you mean?" snapped Oliver.

"Perhaps you should come and see, Mr Drew," said poor Sandra, who just worked in the ticket office in her spare time, and had no idea what might cause a whole zoo full of animals to suddenly – well – *stop*.

Every single animal in the zoo had frozen. They walked past towering statues of giraffes, piles of silent snakes, penguins scattered around like boulders, monkeys hanging from trees like furry fruit. They blinked and they breathed, but not one of them moved. It made the rain seem almost rude, with its hurried droplets and loud pitter-patter.

"They've been like this for two hours,

Mr Drew," said Sandra, wide-eyed. Oliver said nothing. "They all stopped at the same time," she went on, and Oliver carried on saying nothing. "Could it be that lemur flu?" she tried, and Oliver said nothing so aggressively that she blushed

and stopped talking. They walked round the rest of the zoo in silence.

When they reached the end – a butterfly house full of perfectly still butterflies, scattered like sweet wrappers – Oliver finally looked at Erica. "Well?" he said.

"I DID warn you."

"You seriously expect me to believe this is some magical curse?"

"You can believe what you like. They won't move until I tell them to," she said. "A word of advice, Oliver. Make some friends your own size. Children are complicated."

While all the humans stared at Erica, the Elephant gave a rumble too low for any of them to hear. Only the elephants in the zoo knew he was talking. *THANK YOU,* he said, and *Get ready.*

At that moment, a herd of humans in suits burst into the butterfly house, waving notebooks and cameras. "That man works here!" cried one, and they rushed forwards. "Are you the manager? A few quick questions!"

"*Evening Herald*, sir. What caused this?"

"The *Daily Gabble*, sir. Will the zoo stay open?"

Oliver reared up to his full height again. "Who let the press in?" he demanded.

Sandra tried to look as still and innocent as the butterflies, and not like someone who should have been at the ticket office. Erica, meanwhile, began explaining very calmly to the baffled journalists that she had cursed the zoo to make it give back her Elephant, while Miss Pritchett explained to anybody who would listen what a terrible person Oliver was.

Oliver was losing control now. "Don't write down a word they say! Not a word! Who told you to come anyway?"

The journalists shrugged and said they had received a mysterious phone call promising a magnificent scoop. The Officer remembered the phone calls that Erica and Miss Pritchett had asked to make last night, and turned scarlet.

"Well there's no scoop," Oliver yelled. "There's no story; there's nothing to see. Skedaddle."

This was glaringly untrue, so the journalists stayed almost as still as the animals, just racing their pens across paper and clicking their cameras.

Oliver swivelled to face Erica. "Fine.

Just suppose I was to believe you are somehow involved in this. How exactly would I make it stop?"

"Do keep up, Oliver," sighed Erica. "Refuse to take the Elephant."

"But, you silly little girl, some other zoo will just take him instead."

"If they do," said Erica, turning to the journalists to make sure they didn't miss it, "then they will suffer the same fate."

Same fate, scribbled an army of pens, while the Elephant posed happily for photographs.

"Oliver, the animals will move again as soon as the Elephant walks through my front door."

"That's ridiculous," spat Oliver, and

behind him Amy Avis faintly echoed, "Ridiculous." The Officer had gone for a little lie down on a bench round the corner.

"Let me show you then," said Erica. She raised her hands above her head and clapped five times, slowly. Behind her, the Elephant let out a silent rumble: *GO*. Somewhere across the zoo, another elephant **TRONK**ed aloud, and the lions heard him and roared, and the monkeys heard them and screeched, and the butterflies began to flap again. Every animal in the zoo stretched and shook itself into life.

Erica clapped again, five times. The Elephant rumbled his silent rumble: *STOP*. The other elephant **TRONK**ed the message to the zoo, and by the time

she had finished clapping, every animal

was still again. Everyone looked at her

in amazement. For once, she was very

glad that no one ever seemed to realize

that the Elephant did things for himself. Not one human besides Erica and Miss Pritchett had any idea that the animals were simply doing what they had been nicely asked to do.

Oliver had turned very white. "I see," he said, which was a lie. "Right," he added – and then, as an afterthought, "Well." He turned to Amy Avis and almost whispered, "Mrs Avis. I'm afraid I cannot admit this Elephant to my zoo."

Amy Avis nodded silently. No one else moved.

"We'd best be going then," said Miss Pritchett cheerfully. "Any chance of a lift in that van of yours?"

Without pausing for an answer, she

strode off towards the sign that read: EXIT
THIS WAY. PLEASE COME AGAIN.
Erica, the Elephant, Amy Avis and the
crumpled Officer followed, leaving Oliver
alone: a stunned snake surrounded by his
frozen butterflies.

When they were home, Miss Pritchett
and Erica and Erica's Elephant all laughed
until they cried.

The Seventh Chapter:
In which the question is taken to the top

The headlines were full of Erica and her Elephant the next day. *The Morning Whisper* said:

TEN-YEAR-OLD GIRL "FREEZES" ZOO

and the *Daily Buzz* said:

HANDS OFF HER ELEPHANT!

while the *Evening Slump* went with:

TAX CREDIT CHANGES PASSED BY LARGE MAJORITY

because the editor thought that the elephant story was silly. That day, for the first time in its history, the *Slump* failed to sell a single copy.

As you can imagine, no zoo in the country would take the Elephant after that. Amy Avis rang people non-stop for nine hours: every zoo, farm, aquarium, vet, pet shop and house-with-a-large-field that she could think of. No one would have him.

"But it CAN'T stay with a ten-year-old girl!" she exclaimed to Mr Avis over dinner. Mr Avis was a quiet sort of man who had long ago given up asking questions like "Why not?", so he just ate his pie in a quiet sort of way. "I mean, REALLY!" she added, and tutted for good measure.

Try as she might, she couldn't charm or threaten anyone into taking the Elephant. At last, she decided that this was a case beyond her powers. It was time to pass Erica and her Elephant on to the highest authority. She phoned Erica to order her to report to the Minister for the Department of Exotic Animals and Hats, in Bloomsbury, London. "And take that Elephant," she said. "Otherwise we shall arrest you both. You will be picked up at nine o'clock tomorrow."

Erica, Miss Pritchett and the Elephant

held an emergency meeting at Miss Pritchett's kitchen table. There was no denying how hard it would be to run away and hide now that Erica and the Elephant were famous. Besides, Miss Pritchett argued, now that no one else would take the Elephant, there was nothing even the Minister could to. "Either he lets you keep him, or he lets him run wild," she said. "Go there and make your case. Show him that you're a safe pair of hands, and there's no reason why he shouldn't give you a Licence. Lord knows, we've had quite enough drama."

The Elephant **TRONK**ed in agreement. Erica was less sure, but they certainly couldn't run anywhere now without being recognized, so she agreed to try it. Miss Pritchett said she would come along too, to tell them how good Erica was with the Elephant. Because, as she pointed out, no one accepts the word of an elephant, and they often don't listen properly to the words of a child.

The ride to London fascinated the Elephant. He peered out of the van as the telltale marks of the capital began to appear – the round Underground signs, the billboard adverts, the red buses and the streets crammed with shops and offices. Then, as they moved through the city, the view changed to severe white buildings and sleepy green parks. Erica could not enjoy the ride as much as the

Elephant did. She could not shake off the feeling that she was on her way to losing him. She almost wished Amy Avis had come with them: it felt strange and somehow sinister to be in the van without her regular tutting. As it was, they went alone, with Man Number One as driver and security.

The Department of Exotic Animals and Hats was a white building standing between a dentist's and a law firm. It had a brass sign with the department's crest, and a black front door with a brass lion's head for a knocker. Man Number One bashed on the door, which was opened by a woman with an enormous smile. While he went to wait outside in the van,

Erica, Miss Pritchett and the Elephant were led to a dark waiting room. There were wildlife magazines from seven years ago on a coffee table, and some rather wilted flowers. The ceiling was a little too low for the Elephant.

After what seemed an age, the smiling woman sprang into the room, saying, "Erica Perkins?" with alarming enthusiasm. The three of them rose and followed her down a corridor to a black door, propped open by a wastepaper basket. "Miss Perkins, Bert!" she said, with the delighted air of someone saying, "Birthday cake, Bert!" or "Massive waterslide, Bert!". She skipped away again, leaving the trio to confront their new foe.

BERTRAM HUGGINS, said the sign on his door. Bertram Huggins was a balding man with a perfectly round face, and glasses perched on top of his head. He looked up at the three of them rather vaguely. "Ah, yes. The little elephant sorceress. Come in, sit down."

They shuffled inside, but Erica could not see a chair that wasn't covered in piles of paper. The whole office was a mess.

"Erica Perkins, isn't it? I had that awful Avis woman tutting down the phone for hours about you. Your name rang a bell of course." He smiled kindly, without really looking at them. He didn't notice, for example, that the Elephant had quietly got stuck in the doorway, and was now trying to wriggle himself out backwards with as much dignity as possible.

"Um. Really?" said Erica, baffled.

"Yes, yes, of course. I remember drawing up the Licence. I must have

forgotten to put it in the post. But I certainly wrote it." The Elephant fell out of the door with a loud POP and rolled back into the corridor, where he stayed, looking sheepish. Bertram rambled on without noticing. "I know I did, because

I did it while your uncle was still on the phone. He said to me that I mustn't forget, that I had to do it RIGHT NOW! And I said he was a terrible fusspot. But I suppose he was right to worry." And he chuckled as if this was quite a good joke.

Erica stared at him. "You know Uncle Jeff?"

"Oh, yes," said Bertram. "We used to go birdwatching together. I haven't the time for that now of course. Things to do." And he waved his hand at the room full of paperwork, which as far as Erica could tell was spectacularly not being done.

Out of the corner of her eye, Erica saw Miss Pritchett open her mouth to tell Bertram off. It looked like she was preparing for a long speech. Erica shot her a look that clearly said, *Don't you dare.* Much as she wanted to scream in Bertram's silly face for all the trouble his forgetfulness had caused, he didn't look like he was used to being told off, and she wasn't prepared to risk ruining this wonderful, magical chance. She could have a Licence. She could keep the Elephant. So she glared at Miss Pritchett, and Miss Pritchett pursed her lips and stayed quiet.

Bertram took ten minutes to find the right form and five minutes to find a pen. At last, unbelievably, he had signed in all the right places, and Erica Perkins really did have a Licence for the Elephant. He handed it over as if it was just yesterday's newspaper. "Can I help you with anything else, Erica? Your uncle was keen to know how you are doing."

Erica had a hundred questions. *What did Uncle Jeff say? How on earth did you just* forget *my Licence? Do you know that policemen are locking up little girls and their friends in your name?* But in that moment, all that came out was: "Why are you the Department for Exotic Animals *and Hats*?"

Bertram smiled. He opened a tall cupboard behind the desk, and inside were the most awful hats you have ever seen. "Some people," he explained, "wear truly terrible exotic hats. When I took this job,

I added 'and hats' so that I could remove especially bad ones."

"Amy Avis has a horrible knitted polka-dot one. It looks like a tea cosy with measles," Erica told him.

"Is that so?" Bertram's eyes twinkled. "Then I think I had better write her a rather stern letter. I don't suppose she has a Licence for that hat."

"Forgive me for pointing out the elephant in the room," cut in Miss Pritchett, "but – well – he isn't, as it were. Shall we go and tell him the good news?" So they all hurried out to where the Elephant was waiting, looking rather sadly at the posters on the wall. Erica ran up and hugged his massive side.

"Elephant! We got the Licence! You can stay!"

The Elephant **TRONK**ed a HOORAY. But it sounded a bit odd, as if he was also trying not to cry.

"Elephant? What's wrong?"

He **TRONK**ed breezily, as if to say "Oh, nothing", but even Miss Pritchett and Bertram could tell that there certainly was a Something. Erica asked if it was his knee, or the shame of getting stuck in the door, but he shook his head. She looked hard into his eyes but she couldn't think *what* it might be, and he kept trying to pretend he was all right.

"Erica," said Miss Pritchett quietly, "look at the poster." Erica turned around, her back to the Elephant, and saw what he had been looking at. It was a picture of four elephants, three adults and a calf, standing in front of a dazzling pink sky. **ORISSA, INDIA** it said. Erica looked at those elephants in the magnificent sunset for a very long time. She thought about the soft greys of her stony beach, and plastic bags full of cabbage in the broken living room, and how lost the Elephant had looked on her doorstep next to the geraniums.

"Elephant," she said gently. "Do you *want* to come back with me?"

He **TRONK**ed, *Of course*, but a bit too loudly.

"Elephant. If you could go back to India, would you prefer that?"

The Elephant didn't say anything, but looked from the poster to Erica and back again. His trunk waved in a confused sort of way.

"We can arrange that," said Bertram. "I have contacts at a reserve in Orissa. They could look after him and help him find a herd to stay with."

This seemed to confuse the Elephant even more. He shifted from foot to foot and looked pleadingly at Erica, as if he wanted her to decide.

"It's up to you," she said, as steadily as she could. "You can live wherever you want. Really."

The Elephant paused. Then he wrapped his trunk around Erica in a crushing hug.

TRONK, he said. And it was crystal clear to all three of them that he meant, *I have to go home.*

The Eighth Chapter:
Farewells

So he did. They all went back to the house first, and Erica packed up the curtains from the unclejeffsroom for him in case he got cold (because she was a very practical girl, but she didn't know very much about India). The evening before he left, he came to her room and placed a bag at the door with some bread, some crisps and an apple in it. **TRONK**, he said proudly.

She smiled. "Dinner! Thank you."

Miss Pritchett came with them to see him off. He had a ticket for a boat leaving from Dover at 11.30 in the morning. They were early, so they bought some salty chips and ate them while they watched the sea go backwards and forwards. Soothing and familiar. Home – for Erica.

At 11.25 they said their goodbyes, ignoring all the people who stopped to photograph a little girl tightly hugging an Elephant, whom she had a Right to, but loved too much to keep.

"Goodbye, Elephant," she said.

TRONK, he replied, and it meant a great deal more than Erica could ever translate into words.

Epilogue:
A note from Erica

I have just finished reading this to Miss Pritchett, and she got very cross with me. She is 103 years old now, and when she gets cross her face almost folds in on itself. "You can't just stop there!" she said,

"Why not?" I asked.

"Because it isn't The End," she scolded me.

I told her that nothing is ever really The End, and I had to stop the story somewhere. We argued about it for a while, and finally we agreed that I would tell you a little bit about what happened next in an Epilogue, which is a bit like a pudding – you don't need it, but it finishes things off nicely.

She is right that it wasn't The End, of course. It *was* the last time I saw the Elephant. But I ended up studying zoology, and now I am a Professor and a leading expert on elephants, so in a way the Elephant was only The Beginning of *that* story. And I moved in with Miss Pritchett until I left for university, so thanks to the Elephant I made a very important friend. Uncle Jeff came home two years later. We built a door between the two houses and I went between them as I liked. So now I know everything there is to know about birds *and* ants *and* elephants.

It wasn't The End for the Elephant either. I suppose it was The Middle. Before coming to me he lived with his first herd in the wild, and then he gave rides in the city for a while. Then it was his brief spell in England, and finally he made it back to India and found a new herd. So living with me was just the jam in the middle of the cake. From what I know now, I would say he must have been about ten years old at the time, so he still had a good fifty or sixty more years of life ahead of him. It certainly wasn't The End for his story either.

But this isn't the story of our whole lives. This is just the story of when a girl got an elephant – or he got her – for a while. If you want to know the rest, you will have to go to Orissa and find the Elephant with the very slight limp, and ask him. I'm sure he will tell you the same thing that I will: that when you give all your heart to something or someone, that story never *really* ends, because it becomes part of you for ever. But for now – for our small story – this is:

THE END.

TRONK

Facts about elephants

At the end of the story, Elephant moves
to India. Here are some facts about
the elephants he could expect to meet
there.

- There are two types of elephant:
  the Asian elephant and the African
  elephant (Erica's Elephant is an Asian
  elephant).

- Elephants are the largest land
  animals in the world.

- Elephants can't jump!

- An elephant can use its tusks to dig for ground water. An adult elephant needs to drink around 210 litres of water a day (a human only drinks around 2 litres a day).

- An elephant uses its trunk to lift food and suck up water then pour it into its mouth. The trunk has more than 40,000 muscles in it.

- Elephants prefer one tusk over the other – just like people are either right-handed or left-handed!

- Elephants have large, thin ears which help them to cool down in hot climates.

- Elephants can swim – they use their trunk to breathe like a snorkel in deep water.

- Elephants use their feet to listen. Just like in the story, elephants can pick up rumblings made by other elephants through vibrations in the ground.

- Elephants are herbivores (they don't eat meat). They can spend up to 16 hours each day collecting leaves, twigs, bamboo and roots.

- Elephants are very social creatures. They sometimes "hug" by wrapping their trunks together in displays of affection.

- Elephants have greeting ceremonies when a friend who has been away for a long time returns to the group. That means Erica's Elephant probably had a big welcome home party when he arrived back in India!

Acknowledgements

I am very lucky: a lot of brilliant people helped me with this book. In chronological order, my elephantine thanks go to:

Dylan Townley, for sending a text message promising "an elephant festooned with tea" that tickled my imagination. The tea got lost along the way, but the Elephant stuck around and caused havoc. Alice Winn and Julie Sullivan, for giving me crucial encouragement and practical advice. The lovely Bryony Woods, for agreeing to be my agent despite the fact that I got lost on my way to our first meeting, and for being an Unstoppable Force ever since. The terrific team at Scholastic: particularly Lucy Richardson, Sean Williams and Pete Matthews. A large **TRONK** to Lucy Rogers, editor extraordinaire and fellow Hufflepuff, for all her hard work and support. Finally, special thanks to Ashley King for the joyful illustrations, and for drawing me my very own picture of Erica for Christmas.

If I had a trunk, I would use it to try and hug all of you at once.

Sylvia Bishop has recently graduated from
Oxford. She performs comedy, and is one
half of the musical double-act Peablossom
Cabaret. *Erica's Elephant* is her first book,
and she intends it to be the first of many
charming stories for young readers.